Contents: -

The Field of Gold.

Marty stood by his favourite rock and studied the valley below him. Far in the distance he could see a golden glow in the sky, the glow was coming from the field of gold.

'Right, today's the day' he told himself and he ran off to find his best friend Sheldone snail.

Arriving at Sheldone's house Marty knocks on his front door.

'Are you there Sheldone?' he shouts.

The front door opens slowly, standing there in a pair of red and blue pyjamas is a very sleepy looking Sheldone.

'Oh, it's you Marty' he yawned, 'What do you want?'

'I'm going on an adventure today and I wondered if you'd like to join me?' Marty said excitedly.

'Another adventure' sighed Sheldone, 'Where too this time?' he asks.

Proudly Marty tells him he is going to the field of gold.

'You're really going to the field of gold' replies a shocked Sheldone.

'Yes,' confirms Marty, and he asks Sheldone if he wants to join him.

Since they were little, Marty's grandpa had told them hundreds of stories about the infamous field of gold and how nobody had ever ventured there.

'Count me in' replied Sheldone, 'Shall we ask Wallace to join us?'

'As soon as you're ready we'll go and ask him,' said Marty.

Sheldone quickly changes. Then the two of them set off in the direction of Wallace's home.

Ten minutes later they arrive at Wallace's front door, Marty knocks loudly on it.

'Who's that banging on my door at this time of the morning' shouts a grumpy Wallace from an upstairs window.

'It is only us' yells Sheldone.

'Do you want to come on an adventure with us today?' asks Marty.

'What sort of adventure?' asked Wallace.

'We're going to the field of gold' shouts Sheldone excitedly.

'Oh, yes please, count me in.' replied Wallace.

'Great' said Marty, 'Meet us down by the river in an hour.'

'And bring some lunch with you' adds Sheldone.

An hour later they meet at the river's edge.

Marty asks the others to go and find the biggest leaf they can.

'What's the leaf for?' asks Wallace.

'We're going to use it to cross the river' replied Marty.

Sheldone and Wallace disappear into the woods whilst Marty goes in search of a couple of strong twigs that they can use to row with.

Moments later the guys return dragging an exceptionally large oak leaf.

'Will this do?' they ask.

Marty puts the leaf into the water and is pleased to see it floats.

'Hooray' shouts Wallace.

Gingerly they get into the makeshift boat.

'It's a bit wobbly' says Sheldone, struggling to keep his balance.

'You'd better sit down and hold on tight' instructs Marty.

They cast off and the makeshift boat makes it way across the river.

Increasing winds causes the little boat to rock from side to side.

'We're not going to make it' shouts a scared Wallace holding on tightly.

'Yes, we will' says Marty reassuringly, 'Just keep rowing.'

They finally reach the other side. Exhausted they decide to take a rest and eat their lunch.

Marty tucks into his favourite cheese sandwiches which he has cut into triangles.

Sheldone has made himself a large lettuce roll.

While Wallace enjoys a very messy mud sandwich.

Stomachs full, they take a short nap.

After resting they begin the long trek towards the farmer's field.

Climbing up the muddy riverbank and make their way to the edge of the field.

'Look' said Marty pointing to the sky, 'There's the gold.'

High above their heads dangling from a thin stem is a golden object.

Wallace gulps.

'That's extremely high' he says.

'I'll get it down' says Sheldone stepping forward and flexing his muscles.

'I'll shake it down' he says grabbing hold of the stem, he shook it as hard as he could.

But nothing happened.

'Let me have a go' says Wallace.

Wallace gives it a good shake but no matter how hard he tries he cannot dislodge the gold either.

'We'll never get that down' he says scratching his head.

Marty steps forward.

'Leave it to me' he said, and he begins to climb the tall stem.

In no time at all he makes it to the top.

'Can you reach it?' asks Sheldone.

Marty tries to grab hold of the gold, but he cannot quite reach.

He tries again, this time with both hands and manages to grab hold of the gold, and after a small struggle the gold breaks free. Feeling triumphant Marty soon realises that he has let go of the stem and both he and the gold fall to the ground.

Marty hits the floor with a thud.

His concerned friends rush to help him.

'Are you ok?' they ask.

'I think so' replies Marty looking a little dazed.

'Look Marty' shouts Wallace and he points to the piece of gold lying next to him.

'Yippee' shouts Sheldone, 'You've done it, we've got the gold.'

They jump up and down with joy.

'Time to go home with our treasure,' says Wallace.

The others agree so they make their way back to the boat, load their precious cargo onboard and row back across the river.

When they reach the other side Marty jumps out of the boat with the gold.

'Come on you two' he shouts over his shoulder as he sets off towards home.

Sheldone and Wallace chase after him.

Puffing and panting they reach Marty's house.

Out of breath, Marty opens the front door.

'Mum, dad, look what we've got' he shouts excitedly putting the piece of gold on the kitchen table.

Marty's parents notice the piece of corn.

'It's gold' hails Wallace.

Marty's parents look at one another.

'I'm sorry to inform you, but that isn't gold' said Marty's dad.

'Not gold?' replies a puzzled Marty, 'But I remember Grandpa telling me a story that the farmer's field was full of gold.'

Marty's mum explains.

'The field is full of corn, to us animals that is as precious as gold, without we would starve.' she said.

She can see the disappointment on their faces.

'Why don't I use this piece of corn and bake you a crusty corn pie, you must be hungry after such a big adventure.'

'We are' they replied licking their lips.

Twenty minutes later there is a steaming hot pie on the kitchen table.

'What a way to end a great adventure' says Sheldone tucking into a large slice of pie.

Up, up, and away.

Today's the day the valley holds its annual kite competition and while the other competitors are tucked up in their nice, warm cosy beds, Marty is already up and working on his design.

With a dab of paint here and a dab of paint there he adds the finishing touches to what he hopes will be the winning entry. Placing it on the table he stands back to admire his work.

'I'm very pleased with that, it's going to take a special kite to beat this one' he said to himself.

Leaving it on the table to dry he decides to go and check on his fellow competitors.

Outside he checks the weather, It's sunny with a gentle breeze, perfect for today's competition.

As he closes his front door his nose picks up a delicious aroma in the air.

'Cor, what a lovely smell' he says to himself, and he goes off to investigate where the smell is coming from.

The aroma leads him to the home of Hattie Hedgehog, she too is up early. Marty peers through her kitchen window. Hattie is baking corn cakes and berry tarts for the competition. Sat proudly on the sideboard Marty notices the biggest corn and berry cake he has ever seen, this is the prize for today's winner.

'Wow' he says licking his lips, 'I hope I'm the winner today.'

He leaves Hattie to her baking and heads off towards Sheldone's house.

Marty knocks on loudly on his front door 'Knock, knock.'

'Are you home Sheldone?' he shouts.

'Yes, I'm home,' came the reply, 'But you can't come in, I haven't finished my kite yet.'

'Ok' replies Marty, 'I'll see you later.'

And he scampers off towards the home of Wallace worm.

Marty knocks on his door.

'Hi Wallace, can I come in?' he asks.

'No, go away' cries Wallace, 'I'm sorry, but I haven't finished designing my kite yet.'

Marty bids him farewell and he goes in search of Lucy Ladybird.

She too is working hard on her design and politely tells Marty to go away.

'They're all working extremely hard on their designs' Marty thinks to himself, 'I hope their kites aren't as good as mine.'

Marty decides to head home for lunch.

After a quick lunch, he grabs his kite and heads towards the field at the top of the valley.

Stood in the centre of the field on a wooden box is Seymour seagull, Seymour is going to be the judge for today's competition.

Raising a megaphone to his lips, Seymour asks for all the entrants in this year's kite competition to bring their kites and join him in the middle of the field.

Marty, Sheldone, Wallace and Lucy step forward. Finally, their designs are revealed.

Marty has made a triangular shaped kite which he has painted to resemble a wedge of cheese.

Sheldone's kite is circular, he has painted a large yellow snail shell on it.

Wallace has gone for a kite with a long thin body while Lucy has designed a square shaped kite covered in red and black dots.

'Right boys and girls, on the count of three I want you to release your kites, the winner will be the one whose kite climbs the highest' explains Seymour.

'One, two, three, release your kites,' he shouts.

Suddenly the sky is full of wonderfully coloured shapes.

A tug on the kite strings sends the kites twisting and turning. They fly up and down, backwards and forwards and one even does a loop the loop.

'Wow mines the highest' shouts Lucy.

'I'm catching up with you' yells Wallace fighting to control his kite.

Sheldone does not have any such luck, the strong breeze causes his kit to come crashing to the ground.

'You won't be winning this year Sheldone' laughs Marty.

The wind causes Wallace's kite to tangle with Lucy's and they both fall to the ground.

Wallace apologises 'sorry Lucy'.

Realising that his is the only kite left in the competition Marty starts to celebrate.

'Yahoo' he shouts, 'I'm the winner' and he punches the air in triumph.

He is so busy celebrating that he doesn't realise that the freshening winds are lifting him into the air.

'HELP!' he cries looking down at the ground.

'Hold on Marty, we're coming to save you' said Sheldone.

Sheldone instructs Wallace to climb on to his shell.

'See if you can reach him' he orders.

Wallace tries valiantly but cannot reach.

Marty is being lifted higher and higher.

'Lucy, climb on my shoulder's' yells Wallace.

Lucy climbs on to Wallace's back and tries to reach him but sadly Marty is out of reach.

'I can't reach him either' she cries.

Seymour steps forward.

'Stand back everybody' he shouts and with a big flap of his wings he takes to the air.

Seymour climbs higher and higher until he is alongside the frightened little mouse.

'I'm really pleased to see you Seymour 'said Marty holding tightly to his kite string.

'Listen Marty, I want you to be a brave little mouse and let go of your kite,' he said.

Marty looks down at the ground and gulps.

'If I let go, I'll fall' he replies.

'Let go, I promise I will catch you' Seymour said reassuringly.

Marty shuts his eyes and does as he is told.

As promised Seymour swoops beneath him and Marty lands safely on his back.

Holding on to him tightly Marty thanks him.

'You're welcome' replies Seymour.

And with another flap of his wings Seymour changes direction and moments later they land safely back on the ground. Much to the relief of Marty and the spectators watching.

There are pats on the back for Marty and huge cheers for Seymour.

Hattie appears with the corn and berry cake and declares Marty the winner of this year's competition.

'Here you go Marty, you're the winner, I bet you could eat this after that ordeal' she said handing him the cake.

'Thank you, Hattie, but I think we're all winners today' declares Marty and he shares the cake with all his friends.

Buster's blues.

It's a beautiful summers morning and Marty is enjoying a stroll by the river.

The sun is out, the birds are singing and all seemed well in the valley.

But that all changed when Marty heard an incredibly sad noise.

Someone or something was not as happy as he was.

Curious, he pushed his way through the tall grass until he came to an opening. There lying on the ground was a dark figure and it clearly wasn't happy.

Cautiously, he approached the figure.

'I say, are you alright?' he asked.

There was no answer.

Marty crept a little closer and asked again.

'Are you ok?' he enquired.

This time the sad figure heard him and slowly turned towards him.

Marty could see it was Buster the farmer's dog.

'Why are you so sad Buster?' he asked.

Sobbing, Buster informs Marty that he has lost his favourite toy, his ball.

'Don't upset yourself' replied Marty.

'You don't understand Marty, I was having so much fun playing with it, but now it's lost, and I can't find it', Buster sobs again.

'Come on Buster cheer up, I'll help you find it,' said Marty.

Marty's offer of help brings a smile to Buster's face.

'You check the bushes, and I'll check the long grass.' he said.

Buster puts his nose to the ground and begins sniffing around, he checks the bushes and the trees but there is still no sign of his ball.

'It's no use' he weeps, 'I've lost it for good.'

'Don't give up yet, we just need some help to find it' replied Marty, 'Come on, follow me,' he said.

Marty runs into the woods and Buster follows him.

Soon they arrive at Lucy's house, luckily for them Lucy is in her garden talking to Sheldone and Wallace.

'Morning all' said Marty, 'Would you help us please.'

'Who's us?' asks Lucy.

Marty turns and points to a sad looking Buster.

'My friend has lost his ball, we need some help to find it, will you help us?' he asks.

'Of course, we'll help,' replies Lucy.

Buster barks excitedly.

'Where were you when you last had the ball?' asked Wallace.

Buster points to the top of the hill.

'I was up there playing catch, I dropped it and it rolled down the hill, I haven't seen it since,' Buster sobbed again.

'Don't upset yourself Buster, we'll find it' said Sheldone.

Wallace has an idea.

'Why don't we roll ourselves down the hill like a ball then maybe one of us will end up next to it' he suggests.

The others agree and one by one they roll themselves down the hill towards the river.

They all end up in a big heap at the bottom.

'Has anyone found it?' barks Buster.

'Not me' replied a bruised Marty.

'Nor me' replies Sheldone, rubbing his head.

Suddenly, there's a strange noise and the noise appears to be getting louder.

'Can anyone else hear that noise' asked Marty.

'I can' replied Wallace, 'What is it?'

'Quack, quack, quack' went the noise.

'Look over there' shouts Lucy pointing towards the river.

Swimming in their direction is Daisy Duck and she is pushing something with her beak.

'Quack, as anyone lost a ball' she asks.

Buster barks loudly as he is happy to see his favourite toy again.

'The ball must have rolled into the river,' explains Lucy.

'That's why we couldn't find it,' laughs Marty.

Daisy brings the ball to the water's edge.

'Here you go Buster' she says pushing the ball towards him.

Buster picks up the dripping wet ball, happy to be reunited with it he shakes it dry and soaks the others.

'Thanks, Buster' they groan.

In the distance a voice can be heard calling Buster's name.

'Buster, Buster, where are you boy?' calls the voice.

Buster recognises it straight away, the voice belongs to his master, the farmer.

'Woof, Woof, I have to go home now' he barks, and he thanks everybody for their help and heads for home wagging his tail as he goes.

The snow monster.

On a chilly winters morning Marty's head slowly appears from his bedding.

'Brr' he thought, 'It's too cold to get up' so he disappears back under his nice warm blankets.

Downstairs his mum has just put his breakfast on the kitchen table.

'It's time to get up sleepyhead' she shouts up the stairs.

A reluctant Marty crawls out of bed. The chilly morning air makes him shiver.

'Hurry up' shouts his mum, 'Sheldone will be here soon.'

Marty has a wash and ventures downstairs. On the kitchen table is a steaming hot bowl of porridge.

'Make sure you eat it all up' said his mum, 'You'll need that to keep you warm today.'

Blowing the steam off his breakfast Marty asks his mum 'Why is it so cold today?'

'I take it you haven't looked out the window this morning?' she replied.

Marty trudges over to the window wipes away the condensation, he's surprised to see the white landscape outside.

'Cool' he shouts, 'It's snowed.'

Just then there is a knock at the front door.

Marty answers it and is hit in the face with a freshly made snowball.

'Gothca' laughs Sheldone.

'Morning Sheldone' scorns Marty wiping the snow off his face.

'What do you want?' he asks.

'Wallace and I are going to build a sled and we wondered if you'd like to help us?' Sheldone replied.

'That sounds like fun' said Marty grabbing his coat.

'Where do you think you are going young man? Interrupts his mum, 'You're not going anywhere until you have finished your porridge' she said.

'But Mum' protests Marty.

'No buts, sit down and eat your breakfast' she orders.

Marty does as he is told and eats the hot porridge.

Breakfast over, he grabs his hat and scarf and heads out of the front door.

'See you at lunch time, Mum' he shouts over his shoulder.

Sheldone and Marty arrive at Wallace's just as he is putting the final addition to the sled.

'What took you so long?' asks Wallace.

'Sorry Wallace, I had to wait for Marty to finish his breakfast' replied Sheldone.

Wallace has not eaten yet and the thought of food makes his stomach rumble.

'What did you have for breakfast Marty?' he enquired.

'Mum made me eat a bowl of porridge' Marty replied.

The thought of a hot bowl of porridge makes Wallace's tummy rumble again.

'The sled looks great' said Sheldone trying to take Wallace's mind off the thought of food.

'I've just got one more bit to fit' he said.

'This is the final piece' said Wallace fitting the hand brake.

'Is it finished? can we take it for a ride now?' asked Marty.

'Sure, we can' replies Wallace.

They take their places on the sled. Sheldone is to sit at the front as he is the driver, Wallace will sit behind him, he'll operate the brakes and Marty will sit at the back, he will be the engine and will provide all the pushing power.

They drag the sled to the top of the hill and one by one they assume their positions.

Marty digs his heels into the soft snow and begins to push. The sled barely moves, so Marty tries again, this time the sled picks up a bit of momentum and gradually they begin to head downhill.

'Here we go, hold on tight' shouts Sheldone.

'This is great fun' yells Wallace.

'Yippee' yells Marty.

They whizz past Hattie, she is clearing snow from her front garden.

'Good morning, Hattie' they shout.

Hattie turns around but there is no one there.

The sled is now travelling at great speed.

'Watch out for that rock' shouts Wallace pointing at a large boulder in front of them.

Sheldone swerves to avoid it, but it is too late.

'Pull on the brakes Wallace' he yells.

Wallace grabs the brake lever, but it snaps off in his hand.

'It's no use' he says waving the broken lever in the air 'I can't slow us down.'

Marty digs his heels into the snow, but no matter how hard he tries he cannot slow the sled down either.

CRASH! the sled hits the rock and is out of control and heading towards the river.

'Get ready for a soaking' warns Sheldone.

Wallace grabs hold of Sheldone and Marty grabs hold of Wallace.

The sled hits the water.

They are surprised not to get the soaking they expected. The river has frozen over and the sled is shooting across the ice.

Spinning out of control, it narrowly misses Lucy who is on the Ice, skating.

Trying to act cool Marty waves to her, but he is immediately thrown from the sled. Wallace tries to grab hold of him, but he is thrown off also.

Sheldone and the sled are heading for a tree on the far bank.

'CRASH' the sled ploughs into the tree, the impact knocks the snow from its branches.

At the base of the tree a large pile of snow has formed.

Lucy skates over and checks on Marty and Wallace.

'Are you two, ok?' she asked.

The pair nod their heads as they wipe snow off their bodies.

'What happened to Sheldone?' asks Marty.

They follow the tracks from the sled, it leads them to a large pile of snow on the far bank. Cautiously they make their way towards it.

'Sheldone, Sheldone, where are you?' they call.

Suddenly the large pile of snow begins to move.

'Blimey' yells Lucy. 'It's a snow monster.'

Moaning and groaning the pile of snow moves towards them.

Scared, Lucy holds on to Wallace.

'It doesn't scare me' says Marty and he lunges towards the monster poking it in the stomach with the broken brake lever.

'Ouch' cries the monster.

'Hang on, monsters don't say ouch' exclaimed Wallace.

Marty pokes the monster again.

This time a large pile of snow falls to the ground.

The snow monster's identity is revealed, it is Sheldone.

'Oh, it's you Sheldone, I thought you were a snow monster,' said Lucy.

'Me? A monster?' replied Sheldone, shivering.

'You did look like one' said Wallace laughing.

Lucy gives him a big hug as Sheldone shivers again.

'You're freezing' she said.

'I know what will warm you up' said Marty, 'A bowl of my mum's hot porridge.'

The mention of food makes Wallace's tummy rumble loudly.

'Alright Wallace, I'll ask her to make you some too' laughs Marty.

Lucy's big surprise.

Today is a special day in the valley because today it is Lucy Ladybirds birthday, and like most people on their birthday she is waiting for the postman to deliver her post.

Suddenly there's a knock at the front door.

Excitedly she opens it. Stood there in his postman's uniform is Percy the postal pigeon.

'Good morning, Lucy, happy birthday to you' he says handing her a bunch of letters.

'Thank you, Percy,' she replies, and she took her cards inside.

The first card she opens is from Sheldone.

He has written 'Happy birthday Princess' inside it, this makes her feel very happy.

She opens further cards from Wallace, Hattie, Seymour, Marty's parents, and Percy and displays them on the mantlepiece above her fire.

'One, two, three, four, five, six,' she soon realises that she has not received a card from Marty.

'That's funny' she thought, 'It's not like Marty to forget my birthday.'

She is interrupted by another knock on the door.

'That must be him now' she thought.

She ran over to the door and opens it expecting to see Marty stood there, but he isn't instead there's a large bunch of flowers on the doorstep.

As she bends down to pick them up Wallace suddenly appears from behind them.

'Surprise Lucy, happy birthday' he shouts.

'Oh, thank you Wallace, they're lovely' she replies, and she invites him in for a cup of nettle tea.

Wallace declines her invitation.

'I'm sorry' he says, 'I can't I have something very important to do.'

He waves goodbye and leaves.

Lucy takes the flowers inside and puts them in a vase. She is about to put the vase on the kitchen table when there is another knock on the door.

This time it's Sheldone.

'Happy birthday Lucy' he says handing her a large box of chocolates.

'Thank you Sheldone' she said, and she invites him in for a cup of tea.

'Sorry Lucy, I can't stop' he said, 'I've got something very important to do' and he say goodbye to her.

'That's funny' she thought, 'Everyone seems very busy today?'

Next to arrive is Hattie. She hands Lucy a beautiful pink, gift-wrapped parcel.

'Happy birthday Lucy, I've made a very special present for a very special person.' She says handing Lucy the parcel.

Lucy tears off the wrapping paper and opens the box, she expects to find a birthday cake inside, instead, Hattie has made her a beautiful sparkling tiara.

Lucy puts it on and admires herself in the mirror.

'You look beautiful,' remarks Hattie.

But she can see the disappointment in Lucy's face.

'Don't you like my gift?' she asks.

'Of course, I do' answers Lucy, 'But I thought it was going to be my birthday cake.'

'I thought we agreed that Marty was in charge of making your cake this year' Hattie replied.

'We did, but I think he's forgotten my birthday,' said Lucy.

'I am sure he hasn't, I expect he's overslept that's all, I will go and find him,' she said and she leaves.

Lucy puts on the tiara and looks at herself in the mirror.

'It is beautiful' she thought to herself.

She is again interrupted by another knock on the door.

'Who is it?' she shouts.

'It's me, Marty' came the reply.

Excited, she rushes over and opens the door.

Seymour is stood there with a large box, and he is out of breath.

'Happy birthday Lucy' he says, 'I would have been here earlier, but this box is really heavy.'

Lucy's not listening to him, she is too busy looking for someone else.

'Who are you looking for?' asked Seymour.

'I thought I heard Marty's voice' she replied, 'I think he's forgotten my birthday.'

Suddenly the large parcel begins to shake. Marty bursts out of the box holding an exceptionally large birthday cake.

'Surprise Lucy' he shouts' Happy birthday.'

Lucy is left speechless.

'She thought you'd forgotten' said a voice behind a nearby hedge.

'Who said that?' asked Lucy.

Sheldone, Wallace and Hattie appear above the hedge.

'Surprise' they shout.

Lucy is shocked to see them.

'What are you doing here?' she asks, 'I thought you were busy today.'

'We've been helping Marty with your cake, we wanted to give you a big surprise' Hattie explained.

'You certainly have' replies Lucy laughing, 'This has been the best birthday surprise ever,' she said.

Printed in Great Britain
by Amazon